# JOHN LITHGOW

## The Remarkable Farkle McBride

ILLUSTRATED BY

## C.F. PAYNE

**Simon & Schuster Books for Young Readers**

NEW YORK LONDON TORONTO SYDNEY SINGAPORE

*My gratitude to Maestro Jesús López–Cobos
and the Cincinnati Symphony Orchestra for
their help in producing this artwork.*

—C. F. P.

SIMON & SCHUSTER BOOKS FOR YOUNG READERS

An imprint of Simon & Schuster Children's Publishing Division

1230 Avenue of the Americas, New York, New York 10020

Text copyright © 2000 by John Lithgow

Illustrations copyright © 2000 by C. F. Payne

SIMON & SCHUSTER BOOKS FOR YOUNG READERS is a trademark of Simon & Schuster.

Book design by Paul Zakris

The text of this book is set in 22-point Mrs. Eaves.

The illustrations are rendered in mixed media.

Printed in Hong Kong

10 9 8 7 6 5 4 3 2 1

Simon & Schuster Children's Publishing and *The Remarkable Farkle McBride* are proud supporters of the VH1 Save The Music Foundation, a nonprofit organization that restores music education to public schools across the country.

LIBRARY OF CONGRESS CATALOGING-IN-PUBLICATION DATA

Lithgow, John, 1945-

The remarkable Farkle McBride / by John Lithgow ; illustrated by C.F. Payne.

p.  cm.

Summary: The musical prodigy Farkle McBride tries a number of instruments before discovering that conducting the orchestra makes him happy.

ISBN 0-689-83340-7

[1. Musicians—Fiction. 2. Musical instruments—Fiction. 3. Conductors (Music)—Fiction. 4. Stories in rhyme.] I. Payne, C. F., ill. II. Title.

PZ8.3.L6375 Re 2000

[E]—dc21

99-089157

For Ian, Phoebe, and Nate, and, of course, Mary
—J. L.

I dedicate this book to my family
—C. F. P.

Oh, pity the prodigy, Farkle McBride!
No matter what instrument poor Farkle tried,
Whether strumming,
or blowing,
or drumming,
or bowing,
His musical passions were unsatisfied.

When Farkle McBride was a three-year-old tyke,
All freckle-y, bony, and thin,
He astonished his friends and his family alike
By playing superb violin.

He went Reedle-ee

Deedle-ee

Deedle-ee Dee

With all of the strings at his side.

Reedle-ee

Deedle-ee

Deedle-ee Dee

The remarkable Farkle McBride!

But when he was four, Farkle played it no more,
In spite of his parents' beseeching.
He shattered the records he used to adore,
He smashed up his resin, ripped up every score,
He threw fiddle and bow to the living room floor
As he shouted, "Enough of your screeching!"

When Farkle was five, his melodical gift
Once again bore rhapsodical fruit:
The woodwinds inspired his spirits to lift,
And he rapidly mastered the flute.

He went Rootle-ee
Tootle-ee
Tootle-ee Too
With all of the winds at his side.
Rootle-ee
Tootle-ee
Tootle-ee Too
The remarkable Farkle McBride!

But at six Farkle flung his flute into the lake,
Notwithstanding its lyrical trill.
He stamped on the dock till you'd think it would break.
"That's it!" he exclaimed. "I've had all I can take!
That tootling gives me a brutal headache!
It's so wimpy and whiny and shrill!"

When Farkle was seven, a different sound
Rekindled his musical flame:
He became the most expert trombonist around,
And the boulevards buzzed with his name!

He went Vroom-pety

Doom-pety

Doom-pety Doom

With all of the brass at his side.

Vroom-pety

Doom-pety

Doom-pety Doom

The remarkable Farkle McBride!

But at eight he declared, to his parents' despair
(And as everyone else might have guessed),
"I can't stand the trombone, with its *blaat* and its blare!
That racket is more than my eardrums can bear!
So return it or throw it away! I don't care!
I despise it, just like all the rest!"

When Farkle was nine, both his father and mum
Were bursting with pride and affection,
For Farkle learned xylophone, cymbals, and drum—
The entire percussionist section!

He went Boom
Bash
Clang-a-ma Clash!
All the clamor that he could provide.
Tinkle-ee
Bingbong
Bumpety CRASH!
The remarkable Farkle McBride!

But soon he fell prey to his usual gloom,
Despite all the praise and the flattery.
First a sigh, then a sulk, then a frown, then a fume,
Then an earsplitting tantrum that emptied the room.
"I can't take it!" he bellowed. "The crash and the boom
And the clang and the bang of the battery!"

Poor Farkle at ten, howsoever renowned,
Reached the end of his
   musical tether.
But then he discovered his
   favorite sound:
Musicians all playing together.

It happened like this: The conductor caught cold
On the day of a major recital.
"You've got to replace him!" young Farkle was told.
"Your cooperation is vital!"

So he took the baton and he gave the downbeat,
And *KA-BOOM!* the foundations were shaken
By glorious music, bombastic and sweet,
That filled up the hall and spilled into the street;
Music that brought the whole crowd to its feet
From the instruments he had forsaken.

They went Reedle-ee
Rootle-ee
Vroom-pety BANG!
"Bravo!" all the spectators cried!
Deedle-ee
Doodle-ee
Doom-pety CLANG!
The remarkable Farkle McBride!

Since that sparkling night, Maestro Farkle McBride
Conducts all the instruments he ever tried.
His happy heart sings
To brass,
drums,
winds,
and strings,
And remarkable Farkle's at last . . .